WHY SPIDERS SPIN

A Story of Arachne

Retold by Jamie and Scott Simons ▪ *Pictures by Deborah Winograd*

Silver Press

Published by Silver Press, a division of Silver Burdett Press, Inc.
Simon & Schuster, Inc., Prentice Hall Bldg., Englewood Cliffs, NJ 07632.
Printed in the United States of America.
10 9 8 7 6 5 4 3 2 1

Art Director: Linda Huber

Library of Congress Cataloging-in-Publication Data
Simons, Jamie.
Why spiders spin : a story of Arachne / retold by Jamie and Scott
Simons; pictures by Deborah Winograd.
p.   cm.—(The Gods of Olympus)
Summary: Because she boasts that she weaves better than anyone,
Arachne is turned into a spider.
1. Arachne (Greek mythology)—Juvenile literature.   2. Spiders-
-Mythology—Juvenile literature.   [1. Arachne (Greek mythology)
2. Spiders—Mythology.   3. Mythology, Greek.]   I. Simons, Scott.
II. Winograd, Deborah, ill.   III. Title.   IV. Series: Simons, Jamie.
Gods of Olympus.
BL820.A75S55   1991
398.21—dc20   89-77203
ISBN 0-671-69124-4   ISBN 0-671-69120-1 (lib. bdg.)   CIP
AC

LONG, LONG AGO in Greece lived a young peasant girl named Arachne. Her humble family bowed low to honor the gods of Olympus. But Arachne would bow to no one, for she knew she was special in one amazing way.

Arachne was the finest weaver in the land. People traveled far and wide to see her dazzling work.

"See the superb colors! Feel the silky threads. How real her pictures look!" they always said.

One day a tired, old woman stopped, surprised at the great beauty of the weavings.

"What a gift you have! A gift so great could come only from the gods," she said.

"Old woman, my gift is my own," answered Arachne. "I owe thanks to no one. Not even the goddess Athena can weave as well as I do."

The old woman's hand twitched on her cane as she raised a twisted finger at Arachne. Then she spoke in a low, cold voice.

"Listen, child, and mind your tongue," she said. "You will never match the gods, for you are only human."

"Then let Athena come and see my weavings for herself," said Arachne.

At these words, lightning flashed and the earth shook. Ragged clothes became golden armor and the bent cane became a spear of war. The old woman had turned into the goddess Athena right before Arachne's eyes. But still, the girl was not afraid.

"Foolish! Stupid!" roared Athena. "How dare you compare yourself to a goddess! I challenge you to a contest. In one week I will return. Then we will see who weaves the better picture."

Dreaming of victory, Athena returned home to Mount Olympus.

"In seven days I will show Arachne that no one weaves better than I," laughed the goddess.

Now Arachne prepared for the contest. She rose with the sun to find shepherds with the best flocks of sheep. Arachne would use only the finest wool for her contest with Athena.

After shepherds cut the wool, Arachne washed it seven times in fresh spring water. Then she pulled it through fine combs until the wool looked like soft, white clouds.

Next Arachne twisted the wool into yarn with her fingers. Little by little, thread as fine as silk wound around the spindle.

Arachne filled tubs with water to prepare her dyes. She lit a fire beneath each one. Into the boiling water she set brown walnuts, green moss, red leaves, fine spices, and vinegars.

Arachne mixed wonderful colors of brown, green, red, orange, yellow, blue, and purple. Then she washed her woolen yarns in the dye pots and placed them in the sun to dry.

On the day before Athena's return, Arachne set up her loom. She dressed it with a rainbow of threads from the deepest purples to the rosiest reds.

On the day of the contest, the goddess Athena appeared with her magical loom. In seconds, it also glowed with a rainbow of colorful threads.

"Let the contest begin!" Athena proclaimed.

Athena began by weaving a picture of the twelve great gods of Olympus. She showed her father, the mighty Zeus, with his thunderbolts. There were Hera, wife of Zeus, and Demeter, goddess of the harvest. Poseidon, god of the sea, looked out with his flowing waves of hair.

"I can tell tales of the gods too!" thought Arachne.

She began to weave a tale about the god Zeus. But she did not show him as a powerful god. Instead she showed the great Zeus changing forms to play silly tricks on ordinary people.

Meanwhile, Athena pictured herself giving humans the gift of the wonderful olive tree. It gave fruit to eat, oil for cooking, and wood to burn for light and heat.

Arachne wove pictures of Zeus in many forms. She showed him as a swan, an eagle, and a spotted snake.

"How foolish is this god, Zeus!" Arachne thought as she wove her fine yarns.

To frame her pictures, Athena wove a border of olive leaves—the sign of peace and her gift to humans. Then she stood back and smiled at her handiwork.

To frame her pictures, Arachne wove a border of flowers so lifelike that people could almost smell the perfume. Arachne stood back, knowing her weaving was as handsome as Athena's.

"Athena, it's true, isn't it?" asked Arachne. "I DO weave as well as you do!"

Athena stared, surprised at the girl's perfect weaving. But seeing that Arachne had made fun of her father Zeus, Athena felt her anger rise.

In a rage, Athena struck the peasant girl's work. She tore the woven threads until they hung like a tired web around the loom.

"Foolish child," screamed Athena. "Since you like to spin so much, you will spin forever."

Twisting open a bottle of magic water, Athena splashed the poor peasant girl.

In a flash, Arachne's head and body grew small. Her hair fell out and her belly grew fat. Her arms grew longer and longer until at last...

Arachne stood before the goddess Athena, not as a peasant girl, but as a spider with eight long, spindly arms.

"For daring to think you were equal to the gods," Athena cried, "you will spin forever and weave a lonely web."

Frightened, Arachne returned home and climbed up to the roof, hiding herself. There, in a dark corner, she began once more to spin a thread. Using the rafters as her loom, Arachne wove an airy web.

Strong enough to catch an insect, but light enough to blow in the wind, Arachne's web caught the sunlight with dazzling beauty.

From that day on, people have admired the spider's weaving. And to honor the young girl who spun threads as fine as silk, the spider keeps its ancient Greek name—arachnid.